Charlotte
the Baby Princess
Fairy

To Charlotte Stockford and Charlotte Pennington, with love

Special thanks to
Rachel Elliot

ORCHARD BOOKS
Carmelite House, 50 Victoria Embankment, London EC4Y 0DZ
Orchard Books Australia
Level 17/207 Kent Street, Sydney, NSW 2000
A Paperback Original

First published in 2015 by Orchard Books

HiT entertainment

A CIP catalogue record for this book is available
from the British Library.

ISBN 978 1 40834 238 1

1 3 5 7 9 10 8 6 4 2

Printed and bound by CPI Group (UK) Ltd, Croydon, CR0 4YY

MIX
Paper from
responsible sources
FSC
www.fsc.org
FSC® C104740

The paper and board used in this book are made from wood from responsible sources

Orchard Books is an imprint of Hachette Children's Group and published by the Watts
Publishing Group Limited, an Hachette UK company.

www.hachette.co.uk

Charlotte
the Baby Princess Fairy

by Daisy Meadows

ORCHARD

www.rainbowmagic.co.uk

Jack Frost's Spell

I know that babies cry a bit,
But goblin infants never quit!
They seem to love to scream and shout
And spit their soggy dummies out.

Without my sleep I just can't cope.
The magic toy's my only hope!
Let royal babies cry all night,
But make those goblin tots sleep tight!

Contents

A New Baby Girl!

"Jessica is such a beautiful baby," said Mrs Walker, smiling at her friend Emily. "Congratulations!"

"Thank you," said Emily, stifling a big yawn. "She's wonderful, but I wish she would sleep a bit more. She cried all last night!"

Rachel Walker was holding Jessica on her lap. She shook a rattle over her head and Jessica smiled.

"She's so sweet," said Rachel, smiling. "I love her little hairband!"

"Look at her fingernails," exclaimed Rachel's best friend, Kirsty Tate. "I can't believe how tiny they are!"

Mrs Walker, Rachel and Kirsty had come to visit Emily and meet Jessica for the first time. Emily unwrapped the tiny clothes and toy rabbit that they had brought for Jessica.

But even as she was
thanking them, she
yawned again.

"I'm sorry, I don't
mean to be rude,"
she said. "I'm just so
tired."

"Why does she
wake up in the night?"
asked Rachel.

"All new babies have to wake in the
night to drink milk," said Mrs Walker.

"Jessica usually goes straight back to
sleep after her milk," said Emily. "I don't
know why she wouldn't sleep last night!"

Kirsty tickled Jessica and she gave
another smile. Emily smiled too.

"Thank you both for playing with her
so gently," she said to the girls.

"It's lovely to see how much you make her smile."

When they were walking back to Rachel's house, the girls couldn't stop talking about how sweet little Jessica was.

"I wonder if we'll be allowed to babysit for her one day," said Kirsty.

"I expect Emily will be glad of that when Jessica's a bit older," Mrs Walker said. "I hope she sleeps better tonight. I remember how tiring it is to be a new mother."

Rachel laughed. She could hardly imagine herself being a baby!

"Did I keep you awake, Mum?" she asked, putting her arm around Mrs Walker.

"Sometimes," said Mrs Walker with a chuckle. "It was all worth it. I wish I knew a magic spell to make babies sleep, though!"

Rachel and Kirsty exchanged a smile. Their fairy friends would probably know a spell or two! The girls had often visited Fairyland together, and they knew that  there was often magic to be found in the human world too – if they looked carefully enough.

They reached Rachel's house, hurried

inside and kicked off their shoes.

"What are you two going to do after lunch?" Mrs Walker asked, as she took the shopping into the kitchen.

"We haven't decided," said Rachel. "We'll have fun whatever we do!"

"I know you will," said Mrs Walker, smiling at them over her shoulder. "Best friends always do."

The girls ran upstairs and into

Rachel's bedroom. Her window was open, and the curtains were billowing in the fresh spring breeze. They bounced onto their beds and smiled at each other.

"A whole weekend to spend together,"

said Kirsty with glee. "What *shall* we do?"

"There's a family fete in the park this afternoon," said Rachel. "We could go to that if you'd like?"

But Kirsty didn't reply. She was staring

into the corner, where Rachel's dolls'
house stood on a low table.

"I didn't know that your dolls' house
had real lights," she said.

"It doesn't," said Rachel in surprise.

"But there is a light on," said Kirsty.
"Look!"

She pointed at the highest and smallest
window. Something was glimmering
inside.

"That's the nursery," said Rachel. "But
where is the light coming from? I haven't
even got any furniture for that room."

The girls slipped onto their knees in
front of the dolls' house and peeped in
through the window. Rachel gave a little
gasp. The little nursery was filled with
a warm glow. There were ABC pictures
on the walls and pretty mobiles hanging

from the ceiling. And in the middle of the room, a tiny fairy was rocking a crib. She turned and smiled at them.

"Hello," she whispered. "I'm Charlotte the Baby Princess Fairy. Would you like to come in?"

"Yes, please!" the girls whispered, enchanted.

"Knock on the front door and close

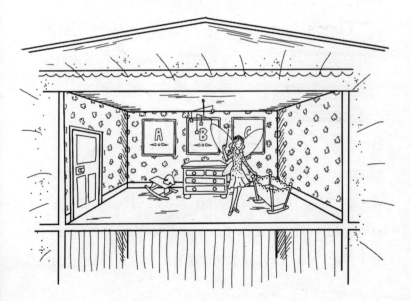

your eyes," said Charlotte.

Rachel leaned down and tapped on the front door. Then both girls squeezed their eyes shut. Something whooshed around them.

"That feels like magic!" Kirsty whispered.

Then they heard the faint click of a door, and they opened their eyes. They were still outside the dolls' house, but

now they were standing on the front step. The house towered above them, and Charlotte was smiling at them from the doorway. They had been transformed into fairies!

Inside the Dolls' House

"Come inside," said Charlotte, holding out her hands.

The girls stepped over the threshold and gazed around in delight. The floor of the hallway was made of real wood, and the wallpaper was decorated with foxes.

"I never realised my dolls' house was so beautiful," said Rachel.

"It's easier to
see the beauty
in things when
you're this small,"
said Charlotte, her
eyes twinkling.

She was wearing a
beautiful flower-print
shift dress and her
brown hair cascaded
in soft curls down
to her shoulders.

"I'm really happy
to meet you," said Rachel. "But what are
you doing in my dolls' house?"

Charlotte led them into the sitting
room and they sat on the tiny doll sofas.

"My job is to make sure that all baby
princesses are happy and comfortable,

and sleep well," Charlotte explained. "I
have a very special magical object to
help me. My soft lion toy always lies in
the crib of the newest baby princess in
Fairyland. But last night, Jack Frost crept
into the Fairyland Royal Nursery and
stole the toy!"

"That's awful!" Kirsty gasped. "How
did you find out that it was Jack Frost?"

"There were icicles still melting in the crib when the baby princess started to cry," said Charlotte. "She cried all night long, but that's not the only problem. If baby princesses don't sleep, next the magic affects baby princes' sleep, and then non-royal babies. So the lost magic of the lion toy has affected all fairy babies, and they have all had a terrible night. It's even started to affect one or two human babies with a special connection to Fairyland."

"That must be why Jessica cried so much last night," said Rachel.

"Will you come with me to Fairyland?" Charlotte asked. "I don't know how to get the lion toy back, and I really need your help."

"Of course we'll help you," said Kirsty,

jumping up. "We won't let Jack Frost make all those babies cry for another night!"

Charlotte fluttered to her feet and waved her wand. The girls heard a far-off lullaby, and then a wave of sleepiness came over them. Their eyes closed as magical sparkles swirled around them, and they felt as if they were being rocked on beds of softest cotton wool.

"Open your eyes," said Charlotte.

Rachel and Kirsty found themselves sitting on a fluffy white cloud, floating above the pink turrets of the Fairyland Palace.

"I want to show you something," Charlotte went on.

The cloud swooped down and hovered beside a toadstool house. Charlotte pointed through the window.

Inside, a fairy mother and father were bending over a crib, where a tiny fairy baby lay crying.

"What's wrong, little one?" the fairy mother said.

"You need your sleep," added the father.

But the baby just kept crying. Rachel and Kirsty hardly had time to catch their breath before the cloud whisked them off to a cottage in a sun-dappled wood. In the garden, another fairy mother was pushing her baby's pram in circles, but the baby inside was still wide awake and crying.

27

"Fairyland is full of tired babies and worried parents," said Charlotte.

She took Rachel and Kirsty from home to home, swooping on the cloud through the Fairyland night sky. From cosy cottages to brick townhouses, they kept seeing the same thing: hundreds of tired fairy babies were wailing, and their parents didn't know what to do.

"I want to help them, but I don't know how," said Charlotte. "How can I even hope to defeat Jack Frost and all his goblins?"

"You're not on your own," said Rachel. "We will stop Jack Frost!"

"The first thing we have to do is fly to the Ice Castle," said Kirsty. "We must find out what Jack Frost has done with the toy lion."

Hand in hand, Rachel, Kirsty and Charlotte left the cloud and zoomed towards Jack Frost's realm.

Locked In!

Jack Frost's Castle looked grimmer and greyer than ever before. There were no goblins patrolling the battlements, and there wasn't a single light on in any of the windows.

"There's something on the door," said Rachel, pointing down to the large entrance.

"It looks like a sign," said Kirsty. "I wonder what it says."

"What if it's a trap?" asked Charlotte in a nervous voice. "Goblins might be waiting for us."

They hovered above the castle for a moment, looking down at the silent castle on the hill and wondering what to do.

"I'll go and read it," said Rachel in a firm voice. "You two stay here. If any goblins do jump out, I know you'll think of a way to stop them!"

She zoomed downwards and landed in front of the door. The sign was written on torn paper in blue crayon. Rachel read it, and then beckoned to Kirsty and Charlotte.

"Look, it says 'Closed for repairs'," she said. "I don't think anyone's at home."

"Where would Jack Frost stay while his home is closed?" asked Kirsty. "He doesn't have lots of friends he could be staying with!"

"I've only ever seen him with the goblins," said Charlotte.

"That's it!" cried Rachel. "I bet he's staying in the goblin village. It's down at the bottom of the hill, and he always makes the goblins help him when he needs something."

The girls knew the way to Goblin Grotto, because they had visited it before. They led Charlotte down the winding, icy path that led to the goblin village.

Ahead, the snow looked grey instead of white, and the squat goblin huts seemed to crouch together. It didn't seem very welcoming.

"Listen," said Kirsty as they got closer.

There was a lot of noise coming from the village. Giggles, gurgles and raspberries filled the air.

"That sounds like a *lot* of happy babies," said Charlotte.

They walked between the huts, and Rachel spotted one with a sign outside the door.

Green Goblin Nursery

Rachel went up on her tiptoes to peep through the window. Inside, she saw seven goblin babies sitting up in a green playpen. Some were giggling so much that they could hardly breathe.

Some were shaking Jack-Frost-shaped rattles, and some were cuddling each other. A female goblin was fast asleep in an armchair, snoring so loudly that the plates on the table were rattling.

"Look at this," Rachel said, beckoning to the others. "I think the goblin babies are finding it hard to sleep too."

Kirsty and Charlotte peered through the window.

"We should disguise ourselves," said Kirsty suddenly. "Fairies are not usually welcome here."

"You're right, they're not," said a sneering voice.

The three fairies spun around and gasped. Six goblins were standing around them in a semicircle. One of them reached forward and snatched Charlotte's wand out of her hand.

"Got you!" he squawked.

The goblins grabbed the fairies and pushed them into the hut opposite.

"No!" cried Rachel.

But she couldn't stop the goblin from closing the door. It shut with a bang, and the key turned in the lock.

"Quick – the window!" Kirsty exclaimed.

But the windows were locked and there was no key. The three fairies stared at each other, feeling helpless.

"How can we get out of a locked room?" asked Charlotte with a groan. "Without my wand, it's impossible!"

"There are some keys on the wall up there," said Kirsty. "It could be one of them."

There were three keys dangling from hooks on the wall, and Kirsty tried all of them with trembling hands. But none fitted.

Rachel bent down and peered through the lock.

"They haven't left the key in the lock," she said, sighing. "I read about how to get out of a locked room in a mystery story once, but the key has to be on the other side of the lock."

Suddenly, Kirsty gave a gasp of excitement. All this talk of locks and keys had given her an idea.

"Goblins aren't always very clever," she said. "If we can get a goblin to open this door, perhaps we can trick him into letting us out."

Giggling Goblin Babies

The fairies made as much noise as they could. Rachel shouted, Kirsty banged pots and pans together, and Charlotte hit the door with a knobbly walking stick she had found in a cupboard. At last, just when they were starting to think that it wouldn't work, they heard a goblin's voice outside the door.

"Well?" the goblin demanded. "What's all the racket about?"

"We don't want to get you into trouble, Mr Goblin," said Kirsty. "We thought you ought to know that there are some door keys inside this hut. If you don't want us to escape, you'd better take the keys away."

There was a pause, and then the fairies heard the sound of keys rattling. Huffing and puffing, the goblin opened the door and walked into the little hut.

Immediately, Charlotte slipped behind him and blocked the doorway.

"Hang on a minute!" the goblin exclaimed.

He stumbled back in surprise and tripped over his own large feet. His legs and arms flailed, and then he landed on his bottom with a loud, painful-sounding thud.

"Quick, let's stop him from getting up!" Rachel exclaimed.

She and Kirsty darted forwards and sat on his legs to stop him from running.

45

Charlotte fluttered forwards and stood in front of him.

"We just want to know if Jack Frost is here," she said. "He has something that belongs to me, and we have come to take it back."

"None of your business!" squawked the goblin. "Get off my legs!"

"We're not moving until you answer Charlotte's question," said Rachel.

"Everyone's being a pain today," the goblin grumbled.

"So, is Jack Frost here?" Kirsty demanded.

The goblin nodded and rolled his eyes.

"He's staying here until the Ice Castle is repaired," he said with a big sigh. He sounded very grumpy.

"Don't you like having Jack Frost as your guest?" Rachel asked.

The goblin folded his arms.

"All he does is complain," he replied. "He wrote a list of all the things that are wrong with Goblin Grotto. Look!"

The goblin pulled out a crumpled piece of paper and showed it to the fairies.

My Complaints, by Jack Frost
1. Bed is too lumpy. I am bruised all over.
2. Food is unpleasant. Sandwiches are not supposed to be green.
3. Ceiling is too low. I have bumped my handsome head too many times.
4. Goblin babies cry too much.

Rachel and Kirsty stifled a giggle. Clearly, Jack Frost wasn't having a very good time either.

"He even brought a special toy to make the babies sleep," the goblin went on. "But it hasn't worked. The babies haven't slept at all. They just keep laughing. They won't stop! No one in the village can get any sleep, the babies are making so much noise."

Rachel and Kirsty looked at Charlotte in excitement. Could the special toy be her magical soft lion? She beckoned to them, and they jumped up from the goblin's legs and darted over to her. The goblin didn't move. He just gave a big yawn and rubbed his eyes.

"That soft toy is what we are looking for," Charlotte whispered.

"But why hasn't it helped the goblin babies to sleep?" asked Kirsty.

"The lion's magic is meant for fairy and human babies," said Charlotte. "Goblin babies are very different."

"The goblins must all be very tired," said Rachel, remembering the goblins she had seen in the Green Goblin Nursery. "I bet they wish they had a magical toy that worked on their babies."

"That's it!" said Charlotte. She turned and kneeled down beside the goblin. "If you will show us where to find Jack Frost, I promise I will make a special magical toy to help the baby goblins sleep."

"Will you help us?" Kirsty asked.

The goblin looked unsure.

"Goblins don't normally help fairies," he said.

"Jack Frost doesn't normally live in Goblin Grotto," said Rachel. "It will make things easier for you if everyone can get a good night's sleep."

The goblin thought about it for a moment, and the fairies watched him anxiously. Would he agree to their plan?

A Frazzled Jack Frost

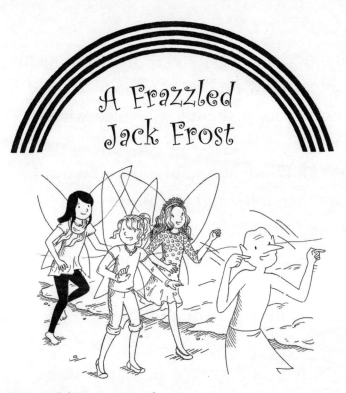

The goblin jumped up.

"Follow me!" he said. "Jack Frost's hut is on the other side of the village."

He darted out through the door. Rachel, Kirsty and Charlotte flew after him, and he led them through winding streets and past rickety huts. As they hurried on, the sound of giggling goblin babies grew louder…and louder…and louder. Soon, the air was filled with gurgles of baby laughter.

"All the goblin babies must be awake and playing," said Charlotte. "I love the sound of happy babies."

The goblin stopped outside a hut with a sign on the door saying 'Guests'. He took a deep breath and knocked on the door.

"Clear off!" barked an angry voice from inside the hut.

The fairies heard a loud clopping noise over the giggles of the babies, and then realised that it was the sound of the goblin's knees knocking together. Rachel reached out, opened the door of the hut and stepped inside. Kirsty and Charlotte

54

followed, with the goblin trying to hide behind them.

The hut was dimly lit inside. All the curtains were closed, and there was a single bed against the far wall. There was a big lump in the middle of the bed. Kirsty stepped forward and pulled the covers back. Jack Frost was hunched over with his bottom sticking up in the air and his hands over his ears. A soft lion toy was tucked under his arm.

"That's it!" cried Charlotte. "That's my magical object!"

Rachel and Kirsty exchanged nervous glances. They knew that they had to be brave, but it was always a bit scary trying to talk to Jack Frost. Holding hands, they stepped forward together and both tapped him on the shoulder.

"Stop!"

Jack Frost exploded upwards, shrieking in fury. He had big purple bags under his eyes, and his spiky hair looked limp.

"Leave me alone!" he yelled, glaring at the goblin next to Kirsty and Rachel. "All I want is a good night's sleep!"

"But it's the middle of the day," said Charlotte.

Jack Frost seemed to notice the fairies for the first time. He looked at the three of them and scowled.

"I will not have fairies in my room!" he bellowed.

He snatched his wand up from a side table and sent a blue lightning bolt crackling across the room. Rachel and Kirsty dived sideways and it crashed into a chair.

Kirsty stood up and looked at Jack Frost bravely. "We just want to talk to you about—"

"I'm not talking to silly fairies about anything!" Jack Frost roared. "Get out! OUT!"

Another lightning bolt crashed towards Charlotte, who had to flatten herself against the ceiling so it didn't hit her.

"Come on!" cried Rachel. "He's not going to listen to us. We have to get out of here before someone gets hurt."

They all dashed outside and slammed

the door shut,
just as another
lightning bolt
hit it from the
inside. They
leaned their
backs against the
door, panting.

"That was a
narrow escape," said the
goblin in a weak voice. "I think I need to
lie down."

"There's no time for lying down,"
said Kirsty. "We have to try to get the
magical lion toy back."

"You promised that you'd make a
special toy to help the babies go to sleep,"
said the goblin, sticking out his bottom
lip and looking sulky.

"I can't make that until I have my wand," said Charlotte.

"If you fetch Charlotte's wand, she can keep her promise," Rachel added.

The goblin scooted off at top speed, while Kirsty turned to the door of the hut and bent down to the lock.

"Jack Frost, listen to me!" she called through the lock. "I know you're tired,

and that's why you took Charlotte's lion toy. But it won't work for goblin babies. That's why they're still not sleeping."

"You're trying to trick me!" Jack Frost shouted back. "I'm not giving you the toy. It's mine now!"

"But the babies are still wide awake," said Kirsty. "Can't you see that it's not working? It's meant for a fairy princess, not for a goblin!"

"It'll start working soon," Jack Frost bellowed. "Anyway, I want to cuddle it in bed.

61

So go back to your silly fairy palace and leave me alone! I don't believe a word you say!"

Kirsty stepped back, biting her lip, and Rachel spoke into the lock in a loud, clear voice.

"Charlotte has promised to make a special toy that will help the goblin babies to sleep," she said. "But she will only do it if you return the lion toy.

You know that fairies always keep their promises. So what are you going to decide?"

And So to Sleep

There was a long pause. Then the
door handle turned, and the door
creaked open a crack. The fairies
moved closer together. What was Jack
Frost going to do?

"Here," he said in a quiet voice. "Take
it and do what you like with it. Just make
those babies go to sleep."

The lion toy was pushed through the crack, and Charlotte took it in delight. As she hugged it, the goblin came bounding towards them with a wand clutched in his hand. He

held it out to Charlotte, and she took it, smiling.

"Now for a little baby magic," she said.

She raised her wand and a glittering spiral of pastel-coloured sparkles swirled from its tip.

"Goblin babies love to giggle.
Wide awake, they crawl and wriggle.
But goblin mums and dads must rest,
So sleeping babies would be best.

My soft toy will close their peepers,
And turn them into perfect sleepers."

The sparkles instantly turned green and
started to swirl faster and faster, clumping
together to make a lumpy shape in
midair. Then, with a final fizz of magic,
they formed a fluffy
toy in the shape of
a bright-green
frog. The frog
dropped into
Charlotte's
waiting hands,
and she passed
it to the goblin.
"Go and give
this to the youngest
baby," she said.

He took it and darted off again. A few minutes passed and the fairies waited in silence. Rachel and Kirsty crossed their fingers. Then, just as they were starting to worry that the magic hadn't worked, they noticed that it wasn't quite as noisy.

"I think some of the giggles and gurgles have stopped," said Kirsty.

Rachel nodded. "It's definitely getting quieter," she said.

A few moments later, all the baby noises had stopped. There was a moment of total peace. Then… PRRRRRRRRRR! PRRRRRRRRRRR! Rumbling snores echoed from Jack Frost's hut, and the walls began to shake.

A crowd of goblins came hurrying towards them down the street, their hands clapped over their ears.

"Stop him!"

"It's too loud!"

"Time for us to go!" exclaimed Charlotte with a smile.

She waved her wand, and they were surrounded by a flurry of twinkling fairy dust. When it settled, the goblin village had vanished from sight, and they were standing in a beautiful nursery. A snow-white crib was rocking in the middle of the room, and under the lacy canopy, the baby princess was still crying.

"Here's your toy, darling," said Charlotte, leaning over the crib and slipping the lion toy in beside the princess.

Instantly, the baby's cries stopped. She snuggled up against the toy and popped

69

her thumb into her mouth. Her eyelids
fluttered, and in a few seconds she was
fast asleep.

Smiling, Charlotte tiptoed over to the
window and gazed out over the toadstool

roofs and leafy forests of Fairyland.

"All the baby princesses of Fairyland
will now be catching up on their sleep,"
she said with a happy sigh. "Soon, all the
other babies will be sleeping too. And it is
all thanks to you."

She turned and put her arms around

Rachel and Kirsty, who hugged her.

"We're just happy that we were able to help," said Kirsty.

"You can always depend on us, if you ever need our help again," Rachel added.

"Thank you," said Charlotte. "I will never forget what you have done for me – and for all the babies of Fairyland."

She lifted her wand and gave them a final wave. Then the nursery faded, and with a sound like far-away bells, they were back in Rachel's bedroom, kneeling in front of her dolls' house and smiling at each other.

"What an adventure!" said Kirsty in delight.

Before Rachel could reply, the bedroom door opened and Mrs Walker came in. She looked very happy.

"Emily has just called," she said, smiling. "Guess what? She thinks that your cuddles did the trick. Baby Jessica is now fast asleep, and that means that Emily can catch up on her sleep too. Isn't that wonderful news?"

"It's the best," said Rachel.

She and Kirsty exchanged happy smiles. They knew why Jessica was sleeping so peacefully.

"Jessica must be a very special baby," Kirsty whispered as Mrs Walker left the room. "Perhaps one day, she will be a friend of the fairies too!"

Now it's time for Kirsty and Rachel to help...

Catherine the Fashion Princess Fairy

Read on for a sneak peek...

"Three cheers for the princesses!" shouted an excited tourist.

Outside the royal gates, Rachel Walker and Kirsty Tate cheered along with the rest of the crowd, and then gazed up at the palace in the heart of the city. The elegant, spiral bars were painted gold, and decorated with tiny silver hummingbirds.

"Isn't it amazing to think that your mum's friend is in there right now, talking to the youngest princess?" said Rachel to her best friend.

Kirsty nodded. Everyone loved the three princesses, but the youngest – Princess

Edie – was their favourite.

"I wonder which room is hers," she said.

"I think it's that one," said Rachel, pointing up at an open window where white curtains were billowing in the summer breeze.

"Bee has such a different life from us," said Kirsty. "I can't imagine what it must be like to be a fashion stylist and help a princess decide what to wear every day!"

"Her house is amazing too," Rachel added. "I wonder what it's like to live in the city."

"We're going to find out this weekend," said Kirsty with a grin.

Rachel and Kirsty were visiting the city for the weekend with Kirsty's parents. They were staying with Bee, who was an old friend of Kirsty's mother from university.

"Bee always has such interesting stories to tell about the princesses," Kirsty went on. "It's so much fun hearing about what their lives are like. She loves Princess Edie best of all."

"I wish she'd hurry up," said Rachel, gazing up at the window with the billowing curtains. "I can't wait to start sightseeing. I want to visit all the most famous places in the city."

The girls were waiting with Kirsty's parents to meet Bee when she had finished in the palace. Mr and Mrs Tate were taking photos of the sentry guard, and Kirsty slipped her arm through Rachel's.

"It's very different from the palace in Fairyland, isn't it?" she said in a soft voice.

Rachel smiled, thinking of the beautiful

pink palace where Queen Titania and King Oberon lived. They had been friends of Fairyland ever since they first met on Rainspell Island, and they loved sharing their magical secret.

"It's exciting being here," said Rachel. "But I hope that we get to see the Fairyland Palace again soon."

"You may see it sooner than you think," said a silvery voice.

The girls jumped in surprise, and then stepped closer to the gate. An exquisitely dressed fairy was standing with her arm around one of the spiral bars.

The little fairy was wearing a flowing dress of green chiffon, with a sparkling belt clasp and delicate lacy sleeves. A tiny pillbox hat was perched at an angle on her head, and her glossy brown hair coiled over her shoulder.

"Hello," she said. "I'm Catherine the Fashion Princess Fairy."

"Hello, Catherine," whispered Kirsty, glancing around to check that her parents weren't watching. "What are you doing here at the palace?"

"I've come to find you," said Catherine, her eyes sparkling as she looked at them. "There's a problem in Fairyland – please will you come and help?"

"Of course we will," said Rachel at once. "But Catherine, we're at the palace! It's one of the busiest places in the whole city – there are people everywhere. How can we be magicked away to Fairyland right under their noses?"

Kirsty turned her head and gazed at all the eager tourists, snapping photographs, pointing at the palace, laughing and joking. Then she looked in the other direction and smiled.

"I've got an idea," she said, pointing to a large postbox at the corner of the palace fence. "Let's slip behind there. It's so big that we'll be hidden from sight."

Read Catherine the Fashion Princess Fairy to find out what adventures are in store for Kirsty and Rachel!

Join in the magic online by signing up
to the Rainbow Magic fan club!

Meet the fairies, play games and
get sneak peeks at the latest books!

There's fairy fun for everyone at

www.rainbowmagicbooks.co.uk

You'll find great activities, competitions, stories and
fairy profiles, and also a special newsletter.

Find a fairy with
your name!